Star Girl Saves the Toys

Jill McDougall

Illustrated by Pedro J Colombo

The children were at school.
They were making a big noise.
WAA!
CRASH!

Sneaky Pete was cross.
"I do not like that noise," he said.
"I will take the toys away."
BANG!

The children went inside.

Sneaky Pete took the toys.
“That will stop the noise,” he said.
HA! HA!

“Who will help us? said the children.
“I will!” said Star Girl.

Sneaky Pete put the toys in his truck.

Star Girl sent out a big net.

"Let me out!" said Sneaky Pete.

Sneaky Pete cut the net.

He ran away from Star Girl!

Star Girl sent out a net.

“You cannot get away now,” she said.

"I will take you back to the school," said Star Girl.

“You can make toys for the children.”

Soon the children had more toys. The toys made *lots* of noise!